Nowhere Else to Turn

I0670956

Nowhere Else to

Turn

By

Matthew Helmke

Stories of the supernatural in Morocco.

For more information about this book or to contact the author please email:
matthew@matthewhelmke.com

Please see the "Final Notes and Thoughts" section at the end of the book for more information about this licensing decision.

First edition, published 2008 by Matthew Helmke.

ISBN: 978-0-615-26419-6

Printed and bound by Lulu, Inc. http://www.Lulu.com

Dedication

This book is dedicated ...

...to Boujmaa and Fatima for their friendship, love and insights into culture.

...to Hanane and other wonderful Moroccans like her for being open and honest, even when talking about difficult topics.

...and to the grumpy guy in the immigration office in Fes, Morocco for forcing me to stretch myself linguistically, culturally, and for providing me with multiple insights into the culture that I never would have had if my interactions with you had been easy or quick.

Acknowledgments

I would like to thank my wonderful wife, Heather, for her encouragement and assistance, especially being willing to sit and chaperone while I interviewed Moroccan women for portions of the background research. That helped make the atmosphere significantly more comfortable, both for the ladies I interviewed as well as for their families.

Thanks go out to the many Moroccans who were willing to discuss the topic of this book with me and share their stories, even when they were nervous to do so. For many, talking about these taboo topics required them to confront fear of rejection, reprisal, and the supernatural realm. It was not easy, but it was certainly appreciated and enlightening.

I would also like to thank those of my friends and colleagues who helped me edit, fact-check and prepare this book for publication, especially T. Aaron Robinette and Corrie Wilson.

You might be interested to know that this book was created and formatted using free software called Open Office, available at openoffice.org, on a computer running a free operating system called Ubuntu Linux, available at www.ubuntu.com.

Table of Contents

Preface

Trapped. Powerless. We have all felt that way from time to time. How we deal with those feelings depends a lot on our personality, our experiences, and our points of view. I find it interesting to observe people as they struggle against the unknown. All of us experience mysterious events in our lives. We ascribe those things to fate, to the will of God, to happenstance, to luck, or to dark and sinister forces, both seen and unseen. To a large extent, our background and philosophy of life will determine who or what gets the credit for the enigmas we encounter.

Every chapter in this book is a complete story in itself. Some are long and some are short. Each is written from a specific and unique perspective, that of the person from whom I heard the tale. Whether you believe in the supernatural or not, whether you find the events I relay credible or fantastic, I think you will find this collection interesting.

Each story is one which was told to me by a real person, someone I met during my travels throughout Morocco. Every single one was told to me as if it were complete and absolute truth.

I do not claim that the enclosed are representative of the majority of Moroccans, nor even the average Moroccan. They may be, and they may not be. One person in particular told me quite emphatically that "everyone in Morocco believes in the supernatural, in sorcery, in witchcraft, in spirits, and jinn[1] and the evil eye, but no one will admit it to you. They are afraid. They are afraid of what you will think, that you will laugh at them. They are afraid of what might happen to them if they start to talk about these things. Maybe a jinn or a sorcerer will hear them and cause them problems. No one wants problems. Everyone believes, even those who do not participate, except to wear five against the evil eye." I can neither confirm nor deny that claim.

The last phrase in that quote refers to a charm, in the shape of the hand of Fatima, the Prophet's Mohammed's daughter. Her hand, with its five fingers, is said to stop the evil eye. It is said that there remains to this day a great amount of right hand and left hand magic in Morocco.

---

1 Jinn are defined in the second chapter, *A Wife from the Mountains*.

This is a belief, one among many, that predates the coming of Islam to this land, and which has never been eliminated. The right hand is said to be capable of doing magic for good for those who have studied and know how to wield the power. The left is capable of great evil, but it is also the hand with the power to stop the evil eye. The charms and symbols, as well as the live act of putting up a hand to stop the evil eye from causing harm, generally use the left hand.

While I do not claim the following to demonstrate or display truly universal beliefs in this country, regardless of what this particular informant said, I do claim that these are stories that would be considered credible by a large number of people I have met in Morocco, and that the people telling them to me were speaking in a manner that was completely honest and forthright in their belief that the stories are true and that they describe actual events from their lives. I believe everyone was convinced of the truth of what they were telling me. Ultimately, however, I will let the reader decide. It is in this spirit that I will recount the stories, with respect toward those who told them, and with no wish to mock, or demean, or patronize.

I confess that I have added to each of these tales. My additions have been in the areas of setting the scene, broadening the characters, and filling out the dialogue. These additions are completely mine and I must shoulder the responsibility for any problems encountered with them. The details and framework for each story remain completely intact as they were given to me and are things for which I can take no credit.

The first story, *The Big Game*, is the only one that I witnessed firsthand. I am the narrator, and Mohamed is a real person. We attended the game in 2003, when I was living in Casablanca.

The Big Game

It was the day of the big game. My friend, Mohamed, came to me and invited me to attend the match with him. One of the two main soccer teams from Casablanca, Raja, was going to play the national team from Senegal.

We approached the stadium about half an hour before the game was to start. Many of the seats were already filled. As we sat down, Mohamed nudged me and pointed.

"Look! The goalkeeper for Senegal is digging! That is bad."

I could see the man crouched in front of the goal he would be defending. He had dug a small hole with his hands and was dropping something in.

"What is it?" I asked.

"They have magic. It is very powerful. He is burying something that will protect the goal and not allow the ball to enter. Our team is in trouble," my friend replied.

"Wait. You are a good Muslim. Surely you don't believe in this sort of thing," I asked.

"Of course I believe in it!" he replied. "How could I not? Sorcery and magic are in the book[2], so I know they are real. We were warned to avoid these things."

I didn't know how to reply, so I just sat back to see what would happen. The game started slowly, with the two teams taking their turns to learn the other team's defense strategy while attempting to penetrate it and score.

_____
2 The Qur'an.

The Moroccan team tried again and again to score. Each shot was blocked by the Senegalese goalie.

"You see?" my friend asked. "Do you see how strong their magic is?"

I could hear despair in his voice. Before I could reply, Senegal scored a goal. The crowd erupted in moans, cries, and a corporate time of mourning. There were shouts and accusations of cheating and rules violations, the usual.

At halftime, the score remained zero to one, in the Senegal team's favor.

A man came by selling handmade sandwiches, made of egg, mayonnaise, and spices on half loaves of French baguettes. Mohamed and I bought and shared one, while I listened to his lament over the power of the sub-Saharan goalie and his occult skills.

"Look, he's doing it again!"

At halftime, the teams switch sides on the field. I didn't notice him dig the old one up, but as I turned to look, I could see the same man digging and placing something in the ground in front of the goal he would defending in the second half of the game.

"We have to find a way to defeat their magic, or we will never win." I could hear the same sentiment murmured over and over in the crowd around us.

The half got underway. Both sides were playing good defense, and the ball never got close to either goal. Then, with about ten minutes left in the game, a boy ran out to the field. He looked to be about twelve years old, and he was being chased by three security guards.

The crowd erupted in an exuberant cheer. My friend elbowed me to get my attention and to make sure I wouldn't miss the excitement.

"Look! He's going to get it!"

Sure enough, the boy ran quickly to the spot where the opposing player had buried his talisman, dug it up, and was nearly off of the field before the security men caught up. As they carried him out of the stadium, the crowd went wild, cheering their support loudly.

At that moment, the Moroccan team scored a goal. A celebration erupted such as I have never seen. Joy was everywhere, the joy of triumph. This seemed greater than a typical celebration over scoring, this was good overcoming evil, a winning of the war, the stadium's Independence Day.

With two minutes left in the game, the Moroccan team scored again. The cheers never ceased, but continued well after the game itself was over.

My friend and I were carried out of the

stadium by a river of people, twenty thousand strong, all flowing to the one exit door that was open and into the streets. We walked a mile through the streets of Casablanca listening to the shouts and jubilation of the victors.

As we did, he repeated over and over, "Did you see? Did you see? They have great power, but we found a way to defeat it!"

A Wife from the Mountains

Life in the mountains is peaceful. Farming here is difficult because of the rocky soil, but it is worth it. Why? Because we are free. We come when we want, we go when we want. No one comes up here to tell us what to do.

Sometimes the Makhzen come, men from the government. They require us to pay taxes and fill out some forms once in a while. Otherwise, they leave us alone. No matter what they tell you in the town below, they don't really rule here. We let them think so and they leave us alone.

This is an empty place. It is quiet. Listen. You can hear a gentle breeze, some birds across the meadow are singing, Si Mohamed's[3] donkey is braying on the next hill, complaining about being loaded up with vegetables to sell in the weekly market down the hill. I don't blame him. I wouldn't want to carry all that weight down the trail either.

Are you hungry? The figs are ripe, and they are very good this year. I'll send Houda out to pick some. Houda! Bring our guest some of the figs off of the tree, and get a bowl of almonds, too. We had a good harvest of almonds. Eat some!

I'm glad you came so early in the day, and particularly at this time. The sun is out. It is a good time of year. Not too hot, not too cold. It is also good that you came on a souk day, when the weekly market is in session. There is a lot of

_____

3 Si Mohamed means Mr. Mohamed and is a title of respect.

activity on the trails today. People are hiking up and down the mountain from miles all around to buy and sell. The activity is good, it keeps you safe. The jinn don't like it when lots of people are around. They always retreat to somewhere more remote on market days.

Did you know that it is dangerous to travel by yourself in these mountains? We all live here as free men, and we take our freedom seriously. We don't want anyone from the outside to disturb our way of life, so we mostly keep to ourselves. We watch out for each other, too. However, our protection is not automatic for an outsider. You came here with Mohammed, so we know you are okay. Don't worry, you will be safe anywhere on this mountain if you are with him. Everyone knows him. Don't ever come here alone. You don't know who lives up here and what they are capable of doing. That's why the government leaves us alone.

I remember when the French were here. That was a long time ago. I was already in my late 20s when we kicked them out, so I remember a lot about their time in the area. They thought they could come in and tell us how to live, how to farm. They thought they could rule here. They were wrong.

You see that hill? Over there, the tall one with the narrow gorge? I watched some of my father's relatives ambush a French patrol right there. You see that mound at the bottom? That is where we buried a French officer who tried to call for their troops to come in and cause us trouble. After that, they didn't come up on our mountain anymore.

Where did they live? Down there. See that hilltop overlooking the town? No, not that one, it's too close. The other one, about two miles from here, right above the town. Yeah, there. On top of that hill is a fortress. It is in ruins now, but when the French were here, it was the home of more than ten thousand of them. They had a prison there, too. My uncle was taken there and beaten. Others were starved and tortured. That's why the place is in ruins. Too much blood was spilled there. People can't live there anymore. The place is haunted now.

The French came in, they told us they knew how to live here. They told us they knew better than us. They said they were more powerful than we are. Well, they had better guns, and they had airplanes, but those only win battles. You can't defeat people like us with something so small as guns and airplanes, not in these mountains. We have something better. We have freedom, and we will fight to the end of time to keep it. We do what we want, when we want, and we take care of our own.

See that mountain there? It has caves in it. The caves are too small to see from here, they are about ten miles away. When the French would come up the mountains to look for us, we could see them a full thirty minutes before they could get to us. They walk and hike a lot slower than us, so sometimes it would take them almost two hours to walk up here. By they time they would arrive, they would find our homes empty and the places deserted.

They didn't know about the caves for a long time. When they found out, they realized they could not get their soldiers to the caves without passing through dangerous places, where we would be able to kill them en route. They didn't even try to come, but they sent their airplanes.

Do you see that broken area on the

mountain? That was caused by bombs from the French airplanes. The caves are still there, and there are lots more that they never found. They couldn't come in and beat us, so they decided to try to hurt us by bombing the caves. Some people died, most survived. We all got angry.

They would come and break things in our houses while we were gone. Sometimes, someone wouldn't get out in time and they would break up the house, destroy the furniture, and kill the animals right in front of the person. Then, they would beat them up so badly they wished they had died, but they didn't. Instead, they made sure the person was just hurt badly, but not in danger of dying. Why? To scare all of us. To try to make us into sheep who would do their bidding. It didn't work. It made our blood rise and the ferocity of our ancestors' warrior roots came back into us. We fought back. We fought in whatever way we could. And the jinn fought with us.

What are jinn? I thought you said you were educated? What sort of worthless things do they teach at universities?

Jinn are spirits. Some are good, some are bad. They are like humans, but without physical bodies. Men were made from dirt, jinn were made from fire. Some of the jinn are believers and follow God, some are apostate and follow only themselves or Satan. They can take physical form, and they can change that form, but they will not remain in any physical form. They are spirits.

No, no, they are different from angels. Jinn are not eternal. They are born, they live, they get married, they have offspring, and eventually, they die. They live a lot longer than people, over many of our lifetimes.

Jinn can live anywhere in the world, but they prefer quiet, solitary places. Sometimes they will live in caves, but they especially like places where there is water, like springs or wells.

They are a lot like us, here on the mountain. They like to be left alone and not disturbed. Usually, if you treat them with respect, they will leave you alone. Jinn and people can live side by side in peace, if they respect each other.

People on this mountain have seen jinn for thousands of years. It isn't as common now, probably because there are a lot more people today than there used to be, and the jinn like to be alone. Most have probably moved on to more remote areas. When I was a kid, there were less than half the number of homes here that there are today, and the town at the bottom of the hill had maybe five thousand people in it.

Of course I have seen jinn! I've seen them hundreds of times with my own eyes. Most of the ones I have seen, that interact with people, are unbelievers. They are evil. You can call them "demons." They like to play tricks on people. They like to scare us and try to make us forget God.

Sometimes jinn will throw rocks at you while you are walking down a trail. Usually, they are just little rocks, pebbles that don't really hurt when they hit, but your heart starts to beat faster and faster and faster. They love to do things like this right at dusk, or later, during the night. I tell people they should always try to be home and inside after dark, if they are here on the mountain.

At other times, jinn will whisper things behind you as you walk by. You won't see anything, but you will hear someone call your name. Maybe they will start to tell you things, like "I know where you have been" or "There is no one at home right now." It's frightening.

There have been times when the jinn have appeared to me, let me see them. I've seen jinn appear in the shape of animals, like goats or sheep or cows, and then heard human voices coming from their mouths. They may choose to take the form of trees, like when you are walking down a path that you know well and suddenly find a tree that was not there before. They sometimes look like rocks, hoping that you will try to pick them up so that they can do something bad to you.

It was about twenty five years ago when my father died. No one wanted to prepare his grave. I was already married and had children to take care of, some were in their middle teens. I was about forty years old at the time. They needed someone to be an example to them, so I decided to take the responsibility and bury my father. It is important in our faith to bury the dead within a day. I dug the grave, laid my father in the hole, and covered him with earth.

I ran into a problem. I didn't have any stones for the top of the grave, to keep it from sinking in or being dug up. I went out looking, even though it was getting late.

When you came to my house, did you see the fig tree along the path, about a quarter mile from here? The one with the spring next to it? Yes, that's the one, the short, wide and oddly shaped one.

I walked up that same path that night, just at dusk, and I saw a stone underneath that fig tree. The stone was perfect. It was large enough to cover much of the grave, yet flat. It would take a lot of work to lift it and move it, but that was exactly what I wanted.

I lifted the stone, slowly because it was very heavy. Suddenly my head felt light, like I had been spinning in circles over and over. I nearly fell down. That's when I noticed that in the ground, where the rock was, there was a hole that I had uncovered.

Out of the hole flew a group of eight or nine horses, all black and very fast. They ran away quickly. Following the black horses was a female jinn. She rose slowly and said to me, "You have awakened me. You have released me from my prison. Now, you must be my husband."

I was scared. I didn't know what to do. I tried to run away, but I couldn't. She was wise and knowledgeable and crafty. Every move I attempted she anticipated and blocked. I was trapped and had to surrender. Her name was

Lalla Fatima[4].

I married Lalla Fatima and agreed that she would be my wife. She was a Muslim jinn and promised that if I was honest with her, that she would help to protect and take care of me. I was not allowed to tell anyone about her other than my human family—my wife, and some of my kids.

She was tall, with dark black features and no face. She didn't have a nose, she didn't have eyes, she didn't have a mouth, just smooth blackness where a face would usually be. We were never intimate in a physical way, but I saw her almost every day for over twenty years.

Lalla Fatima gave me knowledge, showing me new ways to do things and work more effectively. She gave me wisdom and advice and

---

4 Lalla Fatima means Madame Fatima and is a title of respect.

the ability to see and comprehend new ideas quickly, more easily, and in greater detail. She also did other supernatural things for me that I cannot talk about.

Jinn like her are one of the reasons that our people will never be conquered or removed from these hills. I am not the only one who has had an experience like this, and I am not the only one who has benefited from a relationship with one of the jinn, although there are very few who have been married to one as I have.

In return for all she gave me, I gave her companionship. She was a widow. Her jinn husband had died, and her jinn children were all grown and gone. I sat with her. I talked with her. I shared my company with her.

One day, as suddenly as this all started, she disappeared. I haven't seen her in about five years. I don't know if she moved, if she died, or what has happened. Maybe we each met each others needs and the task was done and it was just time for her to go. I don't know. Only God knows.

Hamid's Field

"Hey, where's Hamid? It's time to eat," called Abdelhafid. "Oh, there you are. Why didn't you answer me? I've been looking all over the house for you since I got back from the south field, and here you are sitting on the couch."

Hamid said nothing. He sat still. He didn't blink. He didn't move. Abdelhafid checked for a pulse.

"What's wrong? Are you sick? You aren't warm, and you are breathing. Why won't you answer me?"

Worry crept in to Abdelhafid's heart. This

was so unlike his brother. Most of the time the problem was getting Hamid to be quiet. What could be going on?

Abdelhafid rose to find the others.

"Mother? What's wrong with Hamid?" he asked.

"I don't know. He came in from the north field and just sat down. He hasn't moved and he hasn't said a word," she replied.

From the time they were small children Hamid and Abdelhafid were very close. They would laugh, joke, sing and dance their way through each day. Of the two, Hamid was the most gregarious and had lots of friends.

There was a sound at the door.

"Hamid! Why didn't you finish seeding the north field like I told you?! You were out there all morning, and the task shouldn't have taken more than a couple of hours. What were you doing all day?" It was their father, Mohammed.

No response. Hamid didn't even turn his head to look. That day he ate nothing, said nothing, and never rose from the couch after sitting down.

A week passed, then two. Finally, an entire month had gone by. Hamid had not spoken once during that time, and had barely moved from his seat. He hadn't worked, he hadn't gone out.

"Hamid, eat something. You are wasting away!" his mother pleaded. "Please, my beloved, eat. I don't know what is going on, but no matter what it is, you have to eat."

Hamid drank a little water stoically and returned the cup to the table.

His mother spoke to her husband, "Mohammed, I'm worried. I am really scared that Hamid is going to kill himself by not eating. You have to take him to the doctor."

Hamid's mother pleaded and pleaded for another week until finally Mohammed was able to take time off from the fields, arrange transportation, and take Hamid on the half day journey from the countryside into town to see a doctor.

When they returned late that night, the news was not encouraging.

"The doctor says he can't find anything wrong with him," said Mohammed to his wife and his other son, Abdelhafid. "His body is fine. Something is wrong in his mind or in his spirit."

The family summoned the local fakih[5]. This particular fakih was special because he understood sihhar, witchcraft, and could use his special knowledge and powers to discern what was wrong with Hamid.

The fakih asked a few questions, thought

5 Religious teacher, leader, and local wise man.

for a bit, and looked deeply into Hamid's eyes. He then wrote something down on a piece of paper and gave it to the family. Walking away from where Hamid could hear them, the fakih said, "He has seen a jinn and it has taken him. Take this paper, and dissolve the ink in a cup of water. Give it to the boy and make sure he drinks it." Then the fakih left.

Over the next several years the family spent all of their money, paying multiple fakihs to come, trying remedy after remedy. They took trips, pilgrimages to the tombs of local and distant saints, saying prayers, lighting candles, and leaving gifts. Nothing helped.

After seven years, Hamid walked with a limp. His body became weak and gaunt. His hair grew long, dirty and matted. He always appeared unsettled, nervous. He looked around constantly.

"Where are you taking Hamid?" his

mother called.

"The same place I always take him," replied Abdelhafid, "Back to the north field. That is the only place where he is content and will sit still. Maybe today he will eat a little something while we are there."

"Take some of the lamb tajine with you from last night's dinner. He always used to love lamb."

"I will."

With that, Abdelhafid led Hamid to the north field, taking him by his frail, shriveled, and nearly useless arm.

"The stars are beautiful on Tuesdays," said Hamid.

"What are you babbling about now?" asked Abdelhafid.

"If you look closely, you can see patterns in the wind. There is a great truth there. You should stop to think about it," Hamid continued.

Abdelhafid sighed lovingly, "There, there. That's enough. We will be in the north field in a few minutes. You can rest there."

"Blue is an odd name for a color. Why blue? Would we still think of the sky in the same way if we called it 'shoe' or something else?"

"I don't know, brother. I don't know."

They arrived in the field and sat on a rock, under a tree at the edge, below a small hillside.

"You know, I don't think she will show herself today, brother," said Hamid.

"Who?" asked Abdelhafid.

"You know who," he responded. "She doesn't come when other people are with me. That's okay, though. I want to be with you today. I only seem to be able to keep my thoughts straight out here, and I'm glad you are here to share them with me today."

"Me too," said his brother. "Hamid, when do you think you will get better? Will you be able to help us work the fields again?"

"That's not up to me. She is in charge of that. I only care about what she wants and what she says. I live for my mistress."

"I think I'll call the Aissawa, the sufi brothers. They are said to be able to break connections like she has made with you, Hamid."

"Don't bother, brother. My Lalla Aisha is stronger than the brothers and their chants. No. Until she decides she is done with me, I am hers. Only in her presence am I allowed to think, speak, and interact. She is here, you know. Right now. With us. She won't let us see her, because you are here, but she is here. I know, because I only have peace when she is nearby."

So life went on. Abdelhafid worked the fields each day. His parents spent everything they had to bring Aissawa and Gnoua brotherhoods to the house to chant and pray. They took Hamid to be seen by more and more fakih, to various saints' tombs and festivals, and more. They did everything they knew to do, and everything they were told. Nothing made a difference. In the end, all was spent. They died penniless, leaving only the north field to Abdelhafid, because no one would buy it from them.

Hamid and Abdelhafid lived out their lives in a small shack that Abdelhafid built near the rock, under the tree, beneath the hillside. Hamid spent his days sitting peacefully, staring into space and conversing with his Lalla Aisha. He wouldn't bathe. His hair and beard grew longer and more matted by the day. But, he was content. Abdelhafid worked the fields, growing enough for them to feed themselves, and a little to sell. And time passed.

Boy on an Errand

The day started like any other day. I heard the clock ring, followed by the usual sounds of breakfast being prepared in the kitchen below my room. I rose to get dressed.

Bleary eyed, I washed my face, combed my hair, and tried to brush the cobwebs of sleep out of my mind. The sky was still dark. I heard the call to prayer come over the loudspeaker, "Allahu akbar! Allahu akabar! ..."

I realized that I had just enough time, so I performed my ablutions at home and got dressed quickly, then went to the mosque to pray. It wasn't far, just a five or ten minute walk. Today, I ran.

As I approached the door, I realized that I had worn my good shoes. I didn't want to leave them at the door, because I was sure that I would worry about them being taken while I was praying, and that distraction would invalidate my prayer. To help me concentrate on God, I asked a shopkeeper nearby for a plastic bag. I entered the mosque, putting my shoes in the bag to keep next to me, and went in to pray. They were just beginning, so I was there in time.

After the prayer time, I returned home. The sun was just peeking over the horizon and I knew my mother and sisters would have food ready and waiting. I was right. I sat and ate in silence and began to plan my day.

"First, I'll go to the shop and see what Abdsalaam needs me to get for him." Abdsalaam is my oldest brother, and the head of the family now that my father is gone. "If I have time, I'll go to the cafe later with Simo and Tariq." Those were some of my friends. We love to sit in cafes and talk. We talk about sports, about politics, about the future, and about the weather. We also talk about girls. A lot. But, only when we are sure no one outside of the group is listening.

I drank my juice and rose to leave. "Hamdullah," I said. "Praise God." God is the reason we have food to eat. It is important to remember to praise him for giving it to us.

Abdsalaam was not in a good mood that day. As soon as I arrived, it began.

"You're late!" he growled.

"Forgive me, brother. It is exactly 8:30, the same time I always arrive," I replied, trying to be submissive and gentle, even while daring to contradict him.

"Don't talk back to me! You are lucky I even let you work here you worthless, good-for-nothing, son of a ..."

The irony of him using phrases like that always made me laugh. I tried to stifle it, but one slipped out.

Slap! His hand impacted the side of my head hard enough to leave me unbalanced and dazed. I sat down quietly and tried to keep the tears from appearing. Any sign of weakness would only give an opening to more abuse.

I thought to myself, "If only I was older. If only I was bigger. If only, if only, if only..."

"...and then you must take the envelope to Si Larbi. Don't delay! This is important. Wait there in his office until he gives you something to bring back to me." I realized my brother was talking to me, and that I had missed half of what he said.

In my panic, I couldn't decide whether to ask him to repeat his instructions, to make sure that I did everything right, or not. What would be better? What would be safer? Think fast! Too late.

"Why are you still standing there? Do you need me to hit you again? Go!" Abdsalaam ordered, pointing to the door of the shop.

I ran out the door. Not knowing what to do, I looked at the envelope my brother had given me. It was sealed, with no markings on the outside, and no way to tell what it contained.

Si Larbi lived very far away, all the way across town. I didn't have any money to take a taxi. I didn't even have enough money for the bus. I decided I needed to start quickly. It would take nearly two hours to walk there.

Another of my friends, Rachid, lived in the same part of town as Si Larbi. His house was on the way, so I decided to stop and say, "Hello." It would only take me a couple of minutes, and if he heard that I was so close and didn't stop, he might be hurt.

"Welcome! I'm so glad to see you. Come in. Come in." Rachid greeted me with a huge smile and let me to the sitting room. He stepped out quickly and returned minutes later with a small table, some cookies, and a pot of tea. "Tell me, how are you? What's new? How is your family?" The questions went on and on, one after the other, with no chance to answer the first before the second was spoken.

I smiled and responded in a similar fashion. After completing the ritual, we settled in to a peaceful and quiet posture, each of us relaxed and sitting back in our seats.

"I told my mother to make sure we have enough couscous. You have to join us for lunch today," my friend said. This was more of a polite order than a question.

"No, I can't," I protested. "My brother sent me to take this envelope to Si Larbi and I need to do it quickly."

"Si Larbi? He is on your side of town this morning. He won't be back until after lunch anyway."

We both looked at the clock.

"There is no way you can make it back across town before he leaves to come home. You should stay here, eat with me, and go to his house afterward," Rachid advised.

I tried to protest, to make sure he really wanted me to stay and eat. After the third invitation, I relented. He wanted me to stay, and I was hungry.

We finished the meal around 2 p.m. I thanked my friend profusely, pronouncing blessing after blessing upon him and his family. Then I walked out to door to find Si Larbi.

When I arrived at Si Larbi's house, only the maid was home. She let me sit on the front step, out of the sun, but she would not let me enter the house. I waited.

After what seemed like forever, but was really about two hours, Si Larbi arrived. He saw me and exclaimed kindly, "There you are! I looked all over for you near your brother's shop. You didn't have to come all the way over here. Did you bring it?"

I handed him the envelope. He opened it and frowned. "Didn't you go to the bank first? This is a letter telling them to deposit the money, that is here in the envelope, into my account. You were supposed to bring me the deposit receipt, and I was going to give you an important paper."

Embarrassed, I let out a meek, "I'm sorry. I

misunderstood."

Si Larbi was very gracious and said, "That's okay. I have to be on your side of town again tomorrow. Have it ready for me then and I'll come to the store."

As I walked away, I wasn't sure whether to feel like the luckiest person alive to be treated so kindly, or whether to shake and cry in terror as I imagined what Abdsalaam would do to me. I began the long hike home.

It was late. I thought I would try to save some time by crossing the creek at a place where there were some rocks that stick up, instead of walking all of the way around to the bridge.

It was right at dusk as I approached the water's edge. I stumbled. I almost fell in, but someone grabbed me. I started to thank him, but he didn't let me go. Instead, he gripped my arm more tightly and pulled out a knife.

The man dragged me to a nearby house and roughly threw me toward the door. He ordered me to remove my shoes and go inside. I did. I entered a room with one small window, overlooking a market down the hill.

I began to ponder my fate. What would happen to me? What was going on? I also wondered whether being forced into slavery would be worse than returning to face my brother.

The door locked behind me. I was alone. I heard noises coming from the house next door, and then the call to prayer. Then I heard the screams.

The man returned, dragging behind him a young woman. Her arm was twisted behind her back. He was hitting her and she was screaming, "Don't send me away! Don't hit me!"

He told me to get out and I did. I ran. I

didn't get very far. Just outside the house next door stood an old woman. I pleaded, "Woman, do you know what is happening here? We need to call for help!"

She told me to be quiet. "That man is my son," she said. "Listen, and I will explain everything.

"The woman you saw is his wife, but she is not a normal woman. No, she is not even human. She is a jinn.

"Every evening, at the call to prayer, she changes. One day she is wonderful; polite, kind, and humble. The next day, she is horrible and evil. Every single day she switches.

"You arrived just as the change was about to happen, and she was out near the creek. My son brought you inside to keep you safe. If you had seen the change take place, the jinn may have decided to kill or injure you."

They returned my shoes, brushed me off apologetically, and I walked away stunned. What should I believe? What should I do? What shall I tell my brother?

It was at that moment that I realized it. My envelope was gone. The screams of the jinn behind me kept me from going back to look for it.

The Old Lady's Visit

Aicha rose slowly and hobbled across the room. It was dark, but that didn't really matter. She had been living here so long that she could move around safely with her eyes closed. That was a good thing, too, because her eyesight was failing. It was for this reason Aicha presumed that the world would forgive her dingy home, poor attire, and disheveled hair. If she can't see it, she can't be expected to do a good job cleaning or maintaining it.

"Ohh," she groaned as she thought about the day to come. "If only I weren't so old, this would be easy." She dreamt back to the days of her girlhood, back when she would run, skip and play like a baby sheep, happy and playful in its innocence.

Someone in the government office had asked her last week how old she was. Aicha responded as she always did, "You can read the card." She was referring, of course, to her government issued identity card, which everyone had been required to carry for years.

"Yes, but your card just says, 'unknown,'" replied the confused official.

"Well, if you people, who are paid to know everything, don't know how old I am, then how am I supposed to know?" Aicha responded, with a hint of playfulness and a slight bit of that air of authority that only elderly matrons have. No one argues with an old woman, she thought to herself, especially one as old as me.

Truthfully, no one in the village knew how old Aicha was. She had always been there, it seemed. There was one old man there, the oldest in town with a birth certificate. He was 83, and he remembered Aicha being old enough to take care of him and his sisters when he was a small boy, so she had to be at least eight or ten years older than him. And she looked it.

Whether it is polite to talk about the elderly this way or not, I am merely trying to be truthful. Aicha looked every bit of 90 years old, and perhaps more. She was short, probably much shorter than at the peak of her life. Her weakening and shrinking frame caused her to walk with a bit of a stoop, leaning on a sturdy old stick she used as a cane. She didn't bother with a veil or headscarf anymore and she liked to joke about it saying things like, "What, I'm going to incite some man to lust uncontrollably if I don't wear these? I would like to meet the man who is excited by my thinning white hair and deeply lined face." Most believed she was only half joking.

Today, Aicha was going to visit her relatives, her nieces and nephews, at their home. She had lost track of everyone's name in the newest generation and all the specific details of their lives, but someone in the family was having a birthday, or a circumcision, or some other party.

It was even harder to remember since Aicha had never married and therefore never had children of her own to take care of her in her old age. She had passed from her father, to her brother, to one of her nephews, and later to one of the boys in the generation after that. The people she now called nieces and nephews were actually great or great-great nephews or something like that. She once tried to remember and realized she didn't actually care. It was at that moment that she had decided, and announced the decision, that she would be living on her own for the rest of her days.

Aicha wasn't quite certain whether everyone was sad she had moved out or happy to see her leave. It was true that she wasn't of any use doing housework or helping raise the young children anymore. Then, almost all of them promised immediately to give her a small amount of money each month. It wasn't much, but she always had enough to pay the rent for her small room and to provide for her meager food needs.

So, Aicha went to the party. Upon her arrival, she was guided gently into the sitting room, to a seat of honor in the women's salon. From there, she couldn't see the door, or the window, or the food, or really follow what was going on, but everyone that came to greet her said this was the seat of honor, so why argue?

At that moment, Aicha started. "He's coming! Get ready," she exclaimed loudly. Her shrill voice became quite loud and animated and she began to direct the family with her hands.

"Who is coming, auntie? What's wrong?" the family asked with concern.

"Why, the fakih, of course. He is almost here," she replied in a matter of fact tone.

"Auntie, what are you talking about? Why would the fakih come?" one asked.

"Ask Mohammed, he gave the invitation," she said.

Just then, there was a knock at the door. It was the village wise man, the fakih. Aicha didn't notice, but several of the family members began to stare at her with fear in their eyes. "Go get Mohammed," one said.

Mohammed arrived and greeted the fakih. "Thank you for coming to pray the blessing. We are almost ready."

His family asked him if he had told Aicha about inviting the fakih. "No, of course not. I didn't tell anyone, not even you," was his reply, as he led the old sage into the men's salon.

The music played. The food was served. Time passed. Alternately, Aicha nibbled at her food, talked quietly to anyone who came to greet her, and took short naps. Then the house became quiet. Even from the woman's salon, Aicha and the other ladies could hear the fakih begin to recite from the Qur'an. He chanted slowly, melodically, with a rich and almost sad sounding tone. At one point Aicha interrupted the proceedings from her seat.

"Stop! That should have been a fatha, not a

damma,"[6] she exclaimed, referring to the vowelling of an Arabic word in his recitation. The family rushed to her to quiet her down, but she would not be pacified. She repeated herself, even more loudly the second time. This time, the fakih heard her, to the embarrassment of the entire family.

Quietly he asked, "Is the lady a sage?"

"No, sir," the eldest man in the family replied. "She cannot read nor write a single letter. She has never been to school or studied anything scholarly in her entire life. I'm so sorry, sir, for the interruption. Please forgive her. Please forgive our family for the disgrace. Please continue with the blessing. Please..."

"That's enough," the old man broke in gently. "Bring the old lady in here to me."

---

6 These are the names of two short vowel sounds in Arabic.

Everyone's eyes widened. This breach in protocol was unprecedented. What would the village wise man say? What was he going to do? Would the family be ruined? Embarrassed? A nervous silence ensued as Aicha was led into the man's salon.

"What did you say, madam?" asked the fakih.

"My lord, you made a mistake." Aicha replied politely, yet firmly. "You pronounced a damma in that word, and it should have been a fatha."

"That is quite a scholarly comment for someone who cannot read nor write. When and where did you memorize the Qur'an?" he asked.

"I have not," said Aicha.

"How then can you speak with such authority?"

At this the family broke in, again begging

the sage's pardon for the humbling correction, for the interruption, and for the embarrassment.

"Please, be quiet," he said gently to the others. "The lady is quite correct. I have quoted this passage with the same mistake for years and no one has caught it until now. This lady, Aicha, should be honored and respected as one blessed by God, for it was not through study or memory that she discovered the error, but by something more powerful and mysterious."

The room fell silent. Nervous glances were exchanged everywhere as the family suddenly acted as if they just wanted the ceremony to end.

"May I ask one more time, dear one, how you knew?" prodded the fakih kindly.

Then, a different voice, that of a man, spoke out of Aicha's mouth. "We are believers," it said in a low, smooth tone. "Don't worry, we do not want to disturb anyone's peace. We will be quiet now."

At that, the old woman fell to the ground. She began to tremble wildly, flailing about with her hands and feet and head thrashing. Her face contorted into a grimace.

"Leave her!" shouted the fakih. He began to quote a different passage of the Qur'an over her, expecting that to exorcise the jinn.

At this, the voice speaking from her changed. Now, it was much more gravelly and rough. "No!" it screamed. "She is ours, and you are a fake. You have no authority here. You can't even quote a simple and common passage correctly. You leave!" The shrieks and screams turned into a low, rumbling growl, like that of a large dog who has been cornered.

The fakih continued, getting louder and more intense as he recited.

Yet another voice began to speak from

Aicha's mouth. This one was calmer, more controlled, and spoke in a melodic and smooth tone, with a hint of mockery. "I know that passage, too," it said. Immediately, this voice began to recite the same passage as the fakih, using the same tones, the same inflection, the same rhythm. It was a perfect imitation, except for the addition of a mocking expression on Aicha's face and an "I dare you to continue" look in her eyes.

The fakih stopped and exclaimed, "I will never return to this house or pray over anyone in this family again." With that, he bundled up his things and walked away.

Some of the family chased after him, trying in vain to change his mind, but he had been shamed. That shame would be too much to bear. He would leave and deny the entire incident. It would be the word of a family against the word of a well respected scholar. He would be fine.

The rest of the family divided the chores in the house, cleaning up, resetting the home, and some knelt on the floor next to Aicha.

"What is going on? What do they want with her? What can we do?" they asked themselves, each other, and even the jinn. At first, the only response was silence and continued grimaces, contortions, and spasms. Finally, one asked directly, "What do you want with her?"

"It's not your business..." came the slow, measured, rumbling reply. Then silence.

Suddenly, it was over. As quickly as the episode had begun, Aicha became herself again. "Why am I on the floor?" she demanded. "Help me up. It must be getting late. I have to go home. How did I get in this room?"

"You don't know, auntie?" one of the

younger ones said.

"Don't play games with me, I'm an old woman. You should be ashamed of yourself." Aicha gathered her belongings and hobbled out the door. No one followed.

A Visit at Night

Aaaiieeh! Aaaiieeeeh! Aaiieh!! Houda awoke with a jolt, screaming and trembling in fear. She began to quote and recite the Qur'an repeatedly and loudly. Her sister, Amina ran into the room.

"What happened? What's wrong?" she yelled.

Aaaaiieeeh! Aaaah! and again Houda returned to her Qur'an recitation.

"Tell me! Tell me what is wrong! How can I help?" her sister demanded. By this time the rest of the family had arrived. In the presence of them all, Houda began to describe what had happened.

"I was asleep," she began, "and I felt something. A big, heavy weight laid hold of my feet. It crept up my legs and continued up my entire body until it arrived at my chest. I couldn't breathe. I couldn't speak. I couldn't cry out. I couldn't even move. I was paralyzed and I was trapped. As I felt it move up to my neck, I was certain that death was close.

"I started to recite the Qur'an, first in my mind, and then slowly, as I was able, with my lips. It began silently, but God hears all. Then, I was able to whisper, in a voice softer than a breeze. My heart was beating so loudly in my ears that I still couldn't hear myself. The feeling started to retract.

"I was able to move my head. I knew I had to continue the fight, or I would die. I kept repeating the Qur'an over and over and over.

Anything and everything I could remember, I spoke. It worked. The oppression went away little by little. When you heard me scream, it was the first time I could make any noise out loud, and I regained that ability just as the feeling left my feet and I would start to move again."

Lalla Saida, Houda and Amina's grandmother spoke up. "This was a boubrak[7]. It is very dangerous. You could have been killed. A jinn was sent to you to take you. We must act quickly to keep you safe."

"Mother," interrupted Karim, their father, "No one believes in that garbage. Don't scare them and fill their minds with superstitious nonsense."

"Shh!" she replied quickly. "Hamza fii al ayin." "Five in the eye." It means, "May the hand of Fatima blind the evil eye and protect us." "My

---

7 This is the name for the event.

son, you don't know what you are saying. There are many things in this world which you understand better than me, but not this one. Leave and let me take care of my granddaughters."

Karim sighed. Most of the world may belong to men, but not this part. He wanted nothing to do with witchcraft, jinn and superstition, but there was nothing he could do to combat it. There was also a very small part of him that worried about whether she might be right. "It is best not to get involved with this," he thought to himself, and left.

"Listen to me and I will teach you," began Lalla Saida. "We must get you to a fakih quickly. Today. He can pray and recite over you a spell of protection after making sure that the spirit has gone. Then we will buy a new hamza charm for you to wear and anything else he recommends.

Do you have any money?"

Houda nodded. "I have fifty dirhams."

"Oh no, that's not enough," her grandmother replied sadly and fearfully, "And I don't think Karim will give us any."

Amina quickly interjected, "I have two thousand rials (one hundred dirhams)."

"Perfect. All together we will have enough," sighed a relieved Lalla Saida. "First, let us go to the hammam and do the cleansing."

"Grandmother, I can do wuzu here, why do we need to go to the hammam?"

"No, my child. The lesser ablution is not sufficient. We don't know what the jinn might have done while you were paralyzed. We must be cautious and make absolutely certain you are ritually clean. We must make ghasul al janabah, the greater cleansing, for you."

"Grandma! I'm a virgin. That is not

necessary! That washing is for after sex."

"Trust me, my girl. That is not its only purpose. Come, we must go quickly."

The three of them went to the hammam, the local bath house, to perform the ritual cleansing, Houda, because she needed to, Lalla Saida, because she knew how, and Amina for moral support. It was a quiet time of day and only two other women were in the hammam. That was good, because Houda wasn't sure she would be able to handle the stress of other women seeing her perform this ritual and wondering if she had become a dirty sinner. In truth, no one else even noticed she was there. They were only there for a few minutes, not the typical full morning's relaxation of a standard, weekly visit.

As they exited, Amina asked, "Grandmother, how will we find a fakih to help us?"

"Don't worry, my child. I know a very good sihhar[8] nearby. I have used him many times."

"Grandma!" exclaimed both girls.

"You have had good lives so far and I have been able to shelter you from this world, but it is very real. We have had supernatural help to keep you safe, to get a job for your father, and later a promotion, to protect against sickness, and more. This man can be trusted to help us," explained Lalla Saida.

They walked quickly and quietly the rest of the way through the city. It was only a couple of miles away, and before too long they arrived at a tall, nondescript apartment building.

"This is it?" asked Houda. "Somehow I was expecting something more mysterious

---

8 Sorcerer.

looking, more exotic."

"Don't judge from looks. Water may be held by any jar, not only the most ornamented," replied her grandmother.

They entered and climbed the stairs, three flights to the correct door. There were no markings except for the apartment number. There was no sign and no other way to know who or what might be inside. This was a place to which one only came by introduction or invitation.

Lalla Saida knocked softly. A voice from inside called out, "Who is it?" Quietly she answered, "Those who seek truth and safety." The door opened and the three seekers entered respectfully, as if entering a holy sanctuary.

"Give me your identity card," demanded a young woman.

Shocked, all Houda could think of to reply was, "What?"

"Your identity card. I need it to make your appointment with the master," the girl replied.

"Grandma, this is weird and I feel uncomfortable. Let's get out of here," said Houda. "Why should he need my card and identity info?"

"My child, the sorcerer needs it to confirm you are telling him the truth during the interview."

Just then the girl broke in. "No, I'm just joking. I saw that once on a television show with Lalla Fatima and it always makes me laugh to watch newcomers squirm uncomfortably." She laughed good-naturedly. "You don't need to give me your card. I will need to ask a couple of simple questions, if that is okay."

A little confused, but relieved, Houda nodded. "Go ahead."

The girl asked about her age, where she

was from, her name, and why she had come to see the sorcerer. Houda replied honestly, and a bit more completely than she had intended to do. The three seekers were directed to sit and wait in a salon while the girl who received them went further into the apartment to talk to the master.

A few minutes later the lights dimmed and the girl returned. "The master will see you now. His eyes don't like the light, so I had to turn them down. Please, stay seated and he will come in shortly."

"Ask for deliverance," came a quiet and raspy voice from the hall. "Ask for deliverance," it repeated. Slowly an old man rounded the corner into the room. He was short and frail, wearing the traditional robes of a southern Berber and a turban. His face was deeply lined and his dark eyes were set back deep into his forehead, set off by his short, white beard. He shuffled into the room and again said, "Ask for deliverance" as he was seated opposite the ladies. He stared at them expectantly. It was the grandmother who answered first.

"Deliverance," she said.

Quickly, the two girls repeated after her, "Deliverance."

"Which of you is the one who experienced the boubrak?" asked the old man quietly.

"It was me," Houda replied tentatively.

"Give me your hand my daughter and I will take a look."

She held out her hand to him.

"No, child, not the hand of evil. Give me your right hand, unless you are Fatima herself, the left hand is dangerous and I don't want to touch it," began the old man.

Embarrassed, she withdrew her left hand and gave him the right. "I'm so stupid," she thought to herself, "I have never given anyone my left hand. Perhaps I am inhabited by jinn."

The sorcerer stared at her hand a long time. He traced the lines with the index finger of his right hand, while holding the hand palm up with his left hand under it. Occasionally he made odd grunts and thoughtful sounds. Hmm. Eiee. Hrumph. This didn't make Houda feel good.

"What do you see, my lord?" said Lalla Saida, finally breaking the tension and disturbing the near silence of the room.

"Oh, my sister! This is not good. Our daughter is in great danger. Someone has cursed her. It is good that you came so quickly. Do you have the money?"

Lalla Saida looked at the sorcerer with confidence, "Yes, sir. We brought three thousand rials. It is all we have."

"Very good," he replied. "Give me one

hundred dirhams. You will need the remaining fifty to buy the things I tell you to buy. That will be enough to keep her safe the rest of the week, and give you time to gather together more money. Next week, bring me two hundred and fifty dirhams, and I will make an amulet that will keep her safe forever. For now, this will do."

He motioned to his assistant, the girl that greeted everyone at the door, and she took the money from Lalla Saida.

"Now, my daughter," he said to Houda, "Let us take a closer look. First, repeat after me, and then I need absolute silence. Deliverance."

"Deliverance," they all repeated. This happened two more times, and then the room fell quiet as the man appeared to enter a trance. He swayed back and forth smoothly, rhythmically. His eyes glazed over and he began to speak to the spirits, "Oh, jinn! I adjure you in the name of

Sulayman the great, your master, to tell me all I need to know to help this girl. I appeal to the good among you. Show me how to prevent the evil one, the evil eye, from taking her away to hell." This continued for a full twenty minutes, with alternating requests, demands, and invitations, all aiming to invoke action from among the jinn. He appealed on behalf of the girl, her sister, her grandmother, her other relatives, both living and dead, on behalf of the Prophet Mohammed and on behalf of his daughter, Fatima, on behalf of other saints long dead and other persons whose names had no meaning whatsoever to the ladies.

In the end, he stared at Houda. Then he looked at Amina. Finally, he looked at Lalla Saida and spoke to her in a low, conspiratorial tone, "Woman, you understand. These children do not yet comprehend what is attacking them.

You must be the responsible one. Take them under your wing and protect them. Guide them. Teach them. You must go to the market and buy what I tell you, and prepare it. They won't know how. The responsibility is yours, no one else can carry it for no one else is capable. Are you ready and willing?"

"Yes, by God," she replied seriously.

He gave her a list of things to buy in the marketplace, powder made from a dried toad, a bit of hair from a zebra's hide, and several other exotic and frightening things. "Prepare it as I have instructed you, and use it as I have directed. Come back next week with the money, like I told you. Then we will finish the task."

He rose silently and walked out of the room.

Immediately the lights came on and the spell of the atmosphere and the sorcerer's presence was broken. The girl who welcomed them at the beginning returned and said kindly, "I hope we will see you next week. Come back and all will be well."

The three ladies rose in silence. They looked at one another fearfully. What would happen? Truly no one knew. None of them had the money that was being requested. How would they raise it? Would this be Houda's last week alive? Only God knows.

I Can Tell Your Future

I have never been to a fortuneteller or a sorcerer. Those things are forbidden in Islam. They are from Satan. Good people should not have anything to do with them. Not ever. This is what The Prophet (peace be upon him) said and taught. This is what the holy Qur'an says. This is what is written in the traditions and what is taught by the scholars.

It really doesn't matter anyway. The people who do these things are only doing it because they want money, and there are always ignorant people who are willing to give them money. I don't think there are any real fortunetellers. I don't think the people claiming to be sorcerers and witch doctors have any real power. They mix up potions out of their heads and use smooth sounding words that say nothing. If there has ever been any power in that sort of thing, it has gone out of the universe.

Oh, wait! I did know one girl, when I was still in secondary school. She was a Moroccan Jew, and she claimed she could tell the future. She was from Fez, from the Hassarfati family, but nowadays they call themselves Serfati. I don't know why. I won't tell you her first name. It doesn't matter anyway, she moved to Spain a long time ago. That was the last I knew of her. Anyway, I'll call her Sara.

Sara and I used to spend a lot of time together. We grew up in the same neighborhood. We played together as children, even though she is a Jew and I am a Muslim, we were close friends. We went to the same schools. We attended the same classes. We liked the same boys.

For years, Sara and I would sit together and dream about the future. First, we used to talk about what would happen when the French leave, when they are forced out of Morocco. Mohammed V, then called a sultan, was still in exile, but our families were working together to help him return. Did you know that the independence movement began in Fez? Well, it did. And it was people from Fez that made the French sit up and take notice. It was people from Fez that convinced our countrymen to rebel against the oppressor. It was our city that led us out of bondage.

We felt good in those days. We would talk of what it would be like when our good sultan was returned to us. Did you know that Hitler once sent him a message, while he was still in exile, offering to help return him to power in exchange for all the Jews? Really, he did. Do you know what Mohammed V said in response? He said there are no Jews in Morocco, that there are no Muslims or Arabs or Berbers either—there are only Moroccans. It was the French who used ethnicities and religion to divide us, and it was Mohammed V who helped unite us. Back then, we really believed it. We were sure that in the golden future, there would be no class, ethnic or religious struggles anymore, not for us Moroccans anyway.

So Sara, she and I were nearly inseparable. We would leave our houses early in the morning to meet each other and walk slowly to school, savoring each moment of one another's company. We would meet in class, when possible, or during breaks to chat and gossip about the day's events and the boys we had seen. Oh! We were some of the first to have the privilege of attending school. That was because of our families and the powerful positions they had in the community, as well as the beginning of changes in society. We dreamed that one day, all girls would have the opportunities we were enjoying.

After school, we would walk home together, slowly. Not too slowly, though. If we took too long we would both get in trouble. Our families wanted to be sure to preserve our honor and that of each family, so we couldn't be out and away from supervision for very long.

And then, the best part, every once in a while, maybe once every month or two, we would have a chance for one of us to visit the other at her house. Oh, how we loved those moments! We would arrive, greet all the female elders and sisters, and then run off to hide in a forgotten corner or room to giggle and whisper.

This went on for years. We were best friends from the time we were four or five years old, until we were in our later teen years. Then, we found out something about her that had been hidden and secret for all these years. She was an ifrit, a demon child. What do I mean? Child, who teaches the youth these days? Do you know nothing of what is important in life? Listen, and I'll tell you the rest of the story. Hopefully you will understand.

One day, when we were about sixteen or seventeen, Sara came to my house. My grandmother was ill, and she came to bring her family's greetings and best wishes for a speedy and complete recovery. After that, we went into a room by ourselves. Sara closed the door. That was rare, but not so uncommon that we would get in trouble for doing it. It usually meant she had some especially good gossip about a boy we both liked, or perhaps some sensitive news about a family in the neighborhood.

Instead, she pulled out some cards. I didn't know what they were, or what they were even called. I asked her where she got the pretty pictures. She smiled and called me silly. "Don't you know what tarot cards are?" she said gently. I was terrified, she wanted to tell our future. I protested that this was forbidden, but she interrupted me and told me to give her my hand, my right hand. Since she put the cards away, I thought it would be okay, so I did.

She studied my hand for a while, then she said softly, "I have bad news. I'll tell you that at the end. First, call your sister." When my sister arrived, Sara looked at her hand as well. "Oh, lovely. I have interesting and mostly good news for you."

Sara proceeded to tell my sister that she would marry a Frenchman, move to France, and that she would marry two times. We replied that this was absurd. It is impossible for a Muslim girl to marry a Christian man. It is impossible for a woman to have more than one husband, because it is vital to know who her child's father would be (which is also why it is okay for a man to have more than one wife, you always know who the father of all the children is, but I'm getting sidetracked). It is impossible because our family doesn't know any foreigners, and especially not among the French. Ridiculous.

Sara only replied by telling me to call my brother into the room. This was unusual, and not really acceptable, but times were changing. We thought that maybe it would be okay to allow him into the room with all of us girls. Plus, Sara wouldn't be alone with him, both my sister and I were there.

We called him and he came. She looked at his hand and told us all that he would meet an American woman and move with her to her country. Well, we conceded that it is legal in Islam for a Muslim man to marry a Christian wife, but we still said it was absurd. We did not know any foreigners.

Finally, she looked at me. "I have very bad news for you. Are you sure you want to hear it? You don't have to."

Since we all thought that she was just making things up and playing some sort of silly game, we all agreed that she should tell us her news.

Sara said that I would never get married, that my brother would get married first, and then my sister. Then she said that our grandmother would not recover from her sickness, but would instead die within the week.

All three of us exploded. How dare she come into our house and say such offensive and outrageous things! She insulted my family, she insulted me. I am the oldest. I can see how my brother, a male, might get married before me, but not my sister. Plus, women here always get married young, and men do not marry until they can support a wife and family, so they get married older. The worst was having the nerve to say that our beloved grandmother would die, and to say so in our house! We grabbed her, dragged her to the door, and tossed her into the street, telling her to never return.

You have to be careful with people who are not Muslim. Sometimes, even if they mean well, they start playing with powers they don't understand and it warps them. Sara was always such a wonderful friend. How this could have happened, we did not know. We were not worried about what she said coming true, as we were convinced it was not real, and that if it were, that God and The Prophet (peace be upon him) would protect us because we are true Muslims.

Then grandma died. It was only four days later. We wept and mourned. Sara's family sent word that they would ask the rabbi at the Em Habanim synogogue to say the kaddish for her. We told them not to bother, that we didn't want or need their satanic mysticism in our family. If their daughter could predict the future, she was in league with devils. If she could not, then she was a deceiver and a liar and therefore evil. And in any case, she had insulted our family in our own home. As a result, we cut all ties to her and to her family.

We never heard from them again. I did see

Sara walking to and from school on occasion, but only from afar. Each of us had modified our daily routines so we wouldn't end up crossing paths. I also took the precaution of warning all of my Muslim friends about her, so they would not be affected by her evil. Life went on. We mostly forgot about Sara and her predictions.

About five years later, when my sister was just seventeen, my father brought home someone he met in his work. At this time, Morocco was once again independent. This was good. Things didn't work out quite as we expected, though. We thought that the French would be our enemies for life, that we would kick them out of our country and never allow them or their influence to return. After we regained our independence, we all discovered that we needed their help, their partnership in trade, their expertise in building infrastructure, and so on. We also discovered that there were a lot of French people who were actually happy that we were no longer considered a protectorate or a colony, but that we were governing ourselves. That surprised us, well, it surprised me anyway. I probably shouldn't speak for everybody.

So anyway, my father brought home this engineer. He was a Muslim, but he also had French citizenship. Wow. We were amazed as my sister and I had never heard of such a thing. He had nice eyes. I had my eye on someone else, and my family knew it and were excited about the prospect. However, my sister was unattached and at a good age. The man thought so too, apparently, as he later asked my father about his daughters. He told my father how difficult it is to find a good Muslim girl to marry in France, and how he was interested in finding a wife during his visit. The two men made an agreement, and my sister was happy. She moved to France with him as his wife.

Later, it was discovered that this man was not everything he said he was. In fact, he was not even a believer! The marriage was a false marriage and my sister returned home humiliated and shamed. Because of the man's lies, and our innocence in the situation, people in town quickly forgave the indiscretion and her reputation, while blemished, was restored to a good one.

After a few years, she caught the eye of a merchant from town. He approached our father, who was thrilled that someone wanted his tainted daughter, and she was married again, this time to a true Muslim.

It was around this time that my brother entered the university. He also began to augment his studies by attending English classes at the American Language Center. There were people there from all over the world. One of the instructors was a single American woman. She wasn't particularly beautiful, but she was a Christian and she was nice. Most importantly, she had a blue passport and the promise of opportunities that came with it.

We all encouraged my brother to pursue her as a wife, even though she was actually older than him. Well, The Prophet's first wife (peace be upon him), Khadija, was an older woman. She was even a widow, and a rich one who helped secure his economic security at that time in his life. Why shouldn't my brother follow his example?

It turned out that the American woman loved all the attention my brother paid to her and was quickly enthralled with his charm. They were married by the end of the year, and it wasn't long after that that they found a way to get permission for him to live with her in America, so they moved there.

That was when we remembered what Sara had said all those years earlier. So far, it has all come true, every bit. I am still hoping that she was wrong about me. Do you know anyone who is interested in marrying a 70 year old virgin?

The Magic Shop

Abderrazzaq was angry. He was usually angry, but today was different. This was a larger, more powerful anger. How dare that foreigner come to his shop and ask him questions! He picked up a pink incense stone and threw it. It landed in a bin of dried herbs without the satisfaction of giving the slightest noise.

A steady stream of curses and obscenities flowed through his mind. Of course, none of these would actually be spoken. No. It was too important to maintain appearances and the steady façade of wisdom. The people must not see Abderrazzaq's anger. That could undermine his power, position, and authority. This was not something worth risking over one nosy infidel.

The day had begun normally. Abderrazzaq had risen early. He had gone to the mosque to pray, then he had come to open his shop for the day. And his shop was a special one. This fact was plain for everyone to see. There were very few who understood the power and the potential of his wares, but anyone, even a stupid kaffir who can't even dress himself properly, could tell there was something powerful here.

It was a small shop. No more than fifteen square meters total, less than one hundred fifty square feet. There was barely enough space for Abderrazzaq to enter and move around, but that was okay. No one was actually allowed inside to browse his stock. On one wall was a door, the wall that faced the small street where crowds passed by on foot all day. When the folding, metal door was open, he could hang some of his products, the ones which drew the most attention and which advertised most clearly his purpose, on the door and the walls beside it. People could see he was a seller of magic supplies, a maker of potions, and a man of extreme power and wisdom in the realm of the supernatural.

There were animal skins from zebras, cheetahs and others. Next to them were hanging strings of dried lizards from the desert and a small, open burlap sack filled with dried chameleons. He had cages with live ones and boxes of tortoises from the desert in various sizes. These were necessary for normal activities, but were far more important for their advertising value. Only someone with deep, esoteric knowledge would be able to procure them and know how and when to use them. Abderrazzaq's most prized possessions, however, were kept inside.

Inside. That is where mysteries live. In the dark. In the secret and secluded places. Only the eyes of the enlightened are allowed to see those things in their raw states. No, Abderrazzaq was not willing to talk about what he used or why. He was not willing to talk about his sources. Once a year he would close his shop for a month or so and just disappear. When he would return, it would be with a fresh supply of power for sale.

No one dares to ask Abderrazzaq for specific items. You don't walk in and ask for a chameleon. You come humbly. You describe your problem, your sickness, or what sort of help you are seeking from the spiritual realm. Only after he completely understands the problem, sometimes taking a full hour just to interview a client, will Abderrazzaq offer a solution. Sometimes, he will enter the darkness of the shop's interior. You will hear bottles clanking, a mortar and pestle grinding, and a knife scraping or cutting. In those times, he will emerge with a small and scented pouch to wear around your neck, or a packet filled with a mysterious mixture of dried herbs and animal parts, maybe some filaments of unknown origin, to add to food or drink to be ingested. Other times, he will set an appointment for the client to meet him somewhere else, usually late at night, for special assistance.

What the hell was that stupid farangee thinking? Foreigners and unbelievers do not belong here. They have no business with us. This is not for them. Abderrazzaq could not get them out of his mind, with their pasty white skin, blue eyes, and the audacity to try to take pictures of him, his shop and his supplies. Do they think I will give my secrets away? To them?? The thought appalled him and made him feel a bit nauseous. I would let this knowledge die first. None of my own family know my secrets. You expect me to tell you, an infidel, a dog? He spat at the ground contemptuously as he contemplated the very idea. He couldn't help going over the scene once again in his mind.

He saw them while they were still far off. Foreigners don't usually come to this part of town. When they do, usually they are lost or something is wrong. Wait! These foreigners were being guided by Hassan. That old traitor. Just because he used to be the neighborhood spy, reporting on everyone's actions to the government, he thinks he is somebody. It's been a long time, Hassan. Remember when they fired you? For being drunk? You are as bad as they are. Don't bring that filth here.

"Salaamu Alaikum!" said Abderrazzaq in a

kind, gentle voice, "Peace be upon you, and greetings Mr. Hassan. I see you brought some visitors with you today."

"Wa alaikum salaam," Hassan replied, "And upon you, peace. Yes, these Americans are looking to find the 'real Morocco,' to discover how 'normal people' live, not just the ones you see at the tour bus stops or the fancy resorts. They are interested in your shop."

"I see." answered Abderrazzaq. "Tell them I sell traditional medicine, herbal supplements to help with digestive problems and things like that."

"Tell them yourself. That one speaks Arabic."

Suddenly the blue-eyed, white man broke in, "Salaam, assaidi. Peace, sir. Please forgive the intrusion. May God open for you the doors of Heaven, please tell me what you do here? What is your purpose in this neighborhood? What do you sell?"

Abderrazzaq was taken aback with a short gasp that he hoped no one noticed. He quickly regained his composure and replied, "Sir, I can see you are well educated. How surprising to meet an American who speaks Moroccan Arabic. Darija is not a common language for foreigners. Are you a Muslim?"

"No sir, just someone who lives in this country and likes the people here very much, enough to work hard and learn how to communicate with my friends. So, you are a sort of doctor, a pharmacist, you say?"

"Yes, that is all. There is no magic here. All we do is help people who can't afford to go to the western doctors and use the European medicines. Our goods cost less and work just as well for minor problems. We can't cure cancer, but I can sell you something to help with impotence." Abderrazzaq hoped the foreigner didn't quite grasp the intended insult, and he amused himself while giving it.

"I see. What sort of stomach ailment is eased with hair from a cheetah skin? Is dried lizard of value as a skin crème? Does it somehow cure psoriasis? I can see that it is not especially effective on acne." Thrust, parry, riposte. The battle of the wits had begun. How long would it continue? Would this outsider be willing to go all the way?

"Tell your friend to put his camera away. You may take no pictures of me, of my shop, or of my things. Do what you want elsewhere, but not here. It is forbidden." Abderrazzaq stood firm, but without showing his hand or answering to the issue. He thought, "I underestimated him. He must be a spy, but for who? I can't risk finding out. This battle need not be won. A stalemate will be adequate. Time to turn to stone."

Apparently the foreigner felt similarly. With a quick word to his comrades, he looked back at the shopkeeper and studied him briefly. Abderrazzaq was a short man, short and thin with a worn face, wrinkled and tan like leather. He wore a traditional robe, with a wool cloak over it, because today was a rather cold day. On his head was a knit cotton skullcap, typical of men of his generation. The clothes were old, and slightly worn, but well cared for. The shop was small and dingy, but absolutely packed with merchandise. Looking into Abderrazzaq's eyes, the foreigner knew he would get no further information from this man. Better to let him save face and maintain his respect in the neighborhood. Perhaps some one of the the several other shopkeepers in the area, all of whom have been watching the exchange intently, will be willing to chat a bit.

"Sir, I thank you for your time. If I ever have a friend with a stomachache, and he is in this area, I will make sure to send him to you for help. May God help you," the foreigner said as a polite goodbye.

"May God help you," replied Abderrazzaq, adding under his breath, "to leave quickly and not return."

Pilgrimage

Sa'id was sick. Again. It was frustrating. His family had tried everything in their power to help him get well. He had visited doctors. He had taken medicine. He had followed their diets and regimes to the letter. Nothing helped.

The Bensouda family was not particularly religious. They prayed, when they thought of it, or when people were around. Otherwise, they considered themselves to be modern people, people who believe in science, in philosophy. God has a place in there somewhere, mainly in the cultural foundations of their lives.

What do you do when you have exhausted

the resources of what you know? There was no medicine left, no new procedure or treatment to try. Sa'id was sick, and he was not going to get well, and least not with the help of science and medicine.

It was in the middle of those feelings and thoughts that Sa'id's uncle arrived. He was an old man, well in his 70s or 80s.

"I know what you need. You need to go to visit the saints, offer a sacrifice, and ask them to pray on your behalf to God."

"With all due respect, uncle, I don't believe it that. No one needs anyone to stand between them and God as an intercessor. If a person wants something from God, he should ask God directly," answered Sa'id.

His uncle, Si Abdellah, continued, "I know you, my nephew. I know your whole family. You are good people, but you don't pray. You don't live for God the way you are supposed to live for God. Why would you expect that he would answer, or even listen to your prayers? The saints are good men, blessed by God. They lived lives of devotion and became friends of God. You have been to the doctor. You have prayed to God yourself. We all know the sorcerers and their work is evil. What is left? Ask the men of God, the murabitoon, those tied to God and to the community, to pray on your behalf."

"I wouldn't even know how, uncle. No one my age believes in those sorts of things. I know that when you were young almost everyone believed in them and did as you are suggesting. Today, no one under the age of forty has any knowledge of this. It is a dying belief."

"Come, my boy, and I will teach you. We have much to do."

Sa'id and Si Abdellah began their

preparations for visits to the tombs of Moulay Boushta, Sidi Ahmad Tijani, Sidi Ali Boughalib, Moulay Idriss the First and the Second, Sidi Hamamoush and even Sidi Ali and Sidi Harazem, although the last two made Sa'id laugh a bit inside since their names are all over the country, being used to sell bottled water from the natural springs bearing their names.

"Uncle, there are so many. How can we do it? Plus, it is very expensive to buy and take a sacrifice with us to each place. How shall we ever pay for it all? What does a dead person need with a chicken or a goat anyway?" asked Sa'id.

"The gifts are for the descendants of the saints. It is our way of honoring the heritage and blessing of the saints themselves, by helping to provide for their progeny. Don't worry, Sa'id, God will provide what we need to give." Si Abdellah didn't tell the boy that he had cleaned out his own life's savings to collect enough money to buy candles and sacrifices to offer at each location. "It is time, let us go."

First, they went to the more commonly known and easiest to visit tombs in Fez. At the shrine of Moulay Idriss the Second they entered quietly, bearing a gift of a large candle. They lit it and put it in place as they asked the descendant of the Prophet Mohammed to assist them in their time of need, to please ask God on Sa'id's behalf for healing, for health, and for protection. Even though they knew the path well, it was difficult to get in and out that day. The city had become a tourist site, with people from Europe, America, and more coming to tour and shop as if Fez is part of a living history museum. While they were praying, the two men saw cameras flash from outside the door of the sanctuary and heard the mobs of tourists in shorts and t-shirts jabbering in unknown languages.

"This is all wrong," began Si Abdellah. "This place has been defiled by all the outsiders coming to gawk and stare. There is no baraka left, no blessing. Let's leave."

He and Sa'id walked just a few minutes, twisting through the narrow, tall and winding passageways of the ancient city. When they arrived at the shrine and mosque of Sidi Ahmad Tijani, it was closed. They hunted around the area until they found someone with a key to open the door. As they entered, they were told that they should have come the previous month, during the annual festival for the saint. At that time, there were people from all over, including as far as Senegal and the Sudan. There had been music, chanting and recitations, sacrifices, and prayers. That was the time to come. If they wanted to enter and pray now, that was okay, but they should also plan to return next year for the festival.

The two men sighed. Again, this felt fruitless and frustrating. Empty. Si Abdellah looked at his charge and directed him to pray. They did, performing all of the necessary parts of the pilgrimage rituals. Then they left.

They hoped their visit to the festivals of Sidi Ali ben Hamdoush and Sidi Ahmed Dghoughi, near Meknes, would be better. Those ended poorly.

At these, several people were arrested for entering into homosexual marriages during the festival. This was after the two men had witnessed amazing acts said to display the power of the members of the Sufi sect, the Hamdusha, acts which did not feel holy at all. The Hamdusha would dance and sing themselves into a frenzy, and at the emotional peak of the festivities begin cutting themselves with bits of pottery, even throwing whole pots into the air and allowing the falling pots to land on their heads to cut and injure them further.

The members of the Sufi brotherhood would drink boiling water and offer it to the crowd. They would stick knives into their eyes, and then threaten to do the same to anyone in the crowd that failed to give an appropriate offering.

Some in the crowd would light candles to pray for the blessing of Lalla Aisha, a female jinn, a spirit. This made the men very uncomfortable.

"Uncle," Sa'id began, "I thought these things were outlawed, both by Moroccan civil law and by Islamic law. I can feel in my heart that these things are not good, and I know they are not what you have taught me my whole life. Are we suddenly Shi'a, that we should behave as they do during their mourning of Ali?"

At that moment, a woman became more and more excited, chanting and dancing with increasing fervor. She entered into a trance and fell to the ground, where she began to speak, but with the voice of a man rather than the one she had been using.

"I agree, nephew. We should leave, and quickly. Surely there is a saint somewhere in Morocco that is still celebrated by people interested in more than money and spectacle, and who are unstained by pagan ritual. We will look," answered Si Abdellah.

Their visits to the other shrines ended with similar feelings, though the specific circumstances were different in each case. They visited places near Fez, then in the surrounding region, and even traveled as far as Agadir in the Souss looking for something that was both powerful and real.

In the end, they decided to visit the shrine of Moulay Idriss the First during his moussem. After the bad experience at his son's tomb in Fez, they had not wanted to come, but they were running out of options, and Moulay Idriss is generally honored most highly among the saints in Morocco. This was the father of the man whose tomb they had visited in Fez, one who brought Islam to Morocco, long before the territory bore that name. Back then, the most powerful of the chiefs of the indigenous Berber tribes lived in the decaying Roman frontier city of Volubilus.

Moulay Idriss was the great-grandson of the Prophet Mohammed, the grandson of Mohammed's daughter, Fatima and his nephew, Ali. He had been the heir to the caliphate in Damascus, but there had been a civil war. A disagreement broke out over who was the best person to lead the Muslim community, a descendant of the prophet, or one chosen solely on the basis of their morality. With the split between the Shi'a and the Sunni, and the victory of the Sunni Ummayads, the Middle East became a dangerous place for a descendant of Mohammed to live. He headed west to spread the word of Islam.

When Moulay Idriss arrived at Volubilus, he entered into an accord with the inhabitants, who crowned him their leader and protector against another Arab, Harun al-Rashid of Baghdad, who claimed dominion over this land. Moulay Idriss led everyone in the Berber tribes in politics and in the faith. He started his own city on the hills nearby, surrounded by olive groves. Zerhoun was easier to defend, and better for living, but it was not perfect. One of his enemies from Baghdad eventually sneaked in and poisoned the holy man, who was then buried in his city. His servant led the community until his son, Moulay Idriss the Second, was able to rule.

"Come, my nephew. Let us go and offer a sacrifice at this holy man's tomb," said Si Abdellah. "Surely one so close to the holy prophet, both in deeds and in blood, will be able to help us. So powerful is this great man's baraka that it is said that seven pilgrimages to his tomb are the equivalent of one pilgrimage to Mecca. Perhaps he will plead with God to have mercy on us."

They arrived by taxi in the town, down at the base, the town square at the bottom of the steep hill. Zerhoun is built on two small, very steep hills, with a open area on one side in the center. From this marketplace, one may climb the steep slopes and walkways up, up, up the hill.

Finally, after a difficult climb for an old man and a sick younger one, they arrived at the tomb. The entrance began with a walk down a long, somewhat narrow corridor. The floor was tiled in a diagonal square pattern of marble and stone. The lower portion of the side walls were covered with small, hand cut tiles in a very basic, but attractive pattern. The walls and archways were pure white, with the occasional brass lamp. They arrived at the main entrance to the inner chamber, which welcomed its guests with beautiful marble pillars, most likely salvaged from the ruins of the Roman city. Of course, the open ceiling of the mosque courtyard was edged with the same green ceramic tiles as the roof covering the mausoleum.

The two men entered the shrine in awe. They respectfully performed their ritual prayers and then approached slowly. As they did, they were overwhelmed with emotion, even Sa'id, who still wasn't sure he believed in all this. They felt at peace, and sat along a wall of the mosque to present their requests. With permission, they spent the night there praying. Then they spent a second night, and a third.

It is said that God did have mercy on them, for they never woke up from their sleep that last night. Instead, the people here say God took them to paradise.

The Grotto

Rabat is pretty this time of the year. It isn't too hot. It isn't too cold. There is a nice breeze that comes in from the ocean which lends a sweet fragrance to the air. If you climb up the steps to the gate and enter the Casbah des Oudaias, then pass through to the lookout point above the mouth of the Bouregreg River, you will have a lovely view of Rabat's sister city, Sale.

You may have heard of Sale. It was the embarkation point for raiders, pirates actually, for many years. This river used to be a little bit deeper, and the shallow hulls of the "Sallee Raiders," as they were known by the British and others, were able to navigate upstream. The deeper hulls of the European and American ships they attacked were unable to enter, and were instead trapped by the cannons at Sale and Rabat. That may have been the high point of local power and international influence.

Today our claim to fame is that we have the seat of the government. The King lives here, he has multiple palaces in the area, and this is also the location of the different government ministries, the parliament, and most of the embassies for the nations of the world. Still, some of the ancient ways remain.

There is a cave nearby, a grotto really. It is a very important grotto. It is filled with baraka, with blessing. A woman who comes to this grotto and performs the proper ritual will marry. That is vital to her happiness and survival. At least that is what they tell me.

Who are they? They are my sisters, my aunt, my mother, and even my grandmother. To make absolutely sure they are telling me the truth, I have asked others about this place. Without fail, they all tell the same story. Still, I'm not ready to do it. Even though all the important women in my life say I am getting old, that I am nearly past my marriageable years, I am just not sure whether this will do anything to help.

I'm sorry. I really should step back a bit. You don't know anything about me, about my family, about my situation. How can you possibly understand what I am talking about, and why this is important, unless you know who and what I am?

I am the youngest daughter of the youngest daughter. The last of the line. Everyone else is married. My grandmother and even my mother are widows, and my two brothers take care of them, one each in the brothers' homes. Then there is me. I am the extra burden that each one fights to get rid of. One extra person in each home is welcome, two people means one person too many. They want me to get married so that my husband will be responsible for my safety, for my housing and food, and for my livelihood.

My sisters all mock me. "Look at you," they say, "You are already fifteen years old, and still you do not have a man." I try to respond that this is 2008, that Moroccans are getting married older now, that it is okay to wait until after I finish high school and maybe even study at the university. They tell me I am a selfish little pig. All I want to do is pursue what is best for my future. They tell me a man is what is best for my future, not "stealing from my brothers."

I really don't know what to do. I want my family to love me, or to at least like me, or in the absence of that, to respect me. They don't. Maybe if I do what they say, they might.

It wasn't always this way. When I was young, and my father was still alive, everyone treated me better. I remember times when he and grandpa would take me to the cafe with them and let me sit at the table while they talked about life, politics, and the news of the day. Those were good times. I miss both men terribly.

Oh yes, back then things were different. If someone was mean to me, then dad or grandpa would stick up for me and protect me. They died last year in a fishing accident, something about there being too many people in the boat and it tipped over. Anyway, I don't know much about what happened, but I've never seen that many people fishing in the same boat at the same time. Where would they put the fish? Well, there's nothing I can do about it but mourn.

Ever since then, I am not allowed to talk about them, I'm not allowed to go outside the house without an escort, and sometimes I can't even go out of my bedroom unless I am coming to help with the housework. It seems I have to do most of the housework now. The good side is that there isn't as much anymore since most of the family has moved out, but grandma and mom don't seem to want to do anything. They boss me around all the time. They make me clean, cook, and everything. The only thing they will do is the shopping, because they say they don't want other people looking at me before I am married and out of their hair.

I just remembered a kind of sad and odd story that will help you understand my life. About six months ago, my sister was preparing to be married. She came in to the house and talked for a while with all of us ladies. There was going to be a big party that week at our house to celebrate. Everyone from our family, uncles, brothers, nieces and nephews, even people from out in the countryside were coming. Her soon-to-be husband's family were all coming, too. There was going to be music and food and I was so excited.

On the day of the party, I spent the whole day in the kitchen, helping prepare the lamb, the roasted chickens, the sweets, and everything. I didn't even get to eat, I was so busy. Finally, the time came and our guests started to arrive. I hurried to take off my work clothes and put on my party dress when my mother, grandmother, and sisters all said, "What do you think you are doing?"

I told them I needed to get ready for the party, and they told me I had to stay in the kitchen to take care of things because they were all going out to host the ladies in the woman's party room while the male relatives would be hosting the men in their room.

I complained that I wanted to go with them, and they said there was no way. I was the youngest, and it was therefore my responsibility to take care of everyone. That didn't seem right, but what could I do?

I heard the music. I saw the presents pass by the kitchen on their way to the room where they were being stored. I finished preparing the food, just like I was told, and gave it to the the relatives in charge of doing the public hosting when they came to take it to the guests. The men ate first. The women ate later. I was allowed to eat whatever was left over. Then, I cleaned it all up by myself and went to bed crying.

Maybe getting married wouldn't be so bad. How am I supposed to meet someone when I am only allowed to go to school and straight home? With how my family treats me, I'm afraid of who they would pick for me. I don't think there have been any men asking for my hand anyway. I wonder, is it me? Is there something wrong with me that no one wants me?

My sisters always call me names and say that I am ugly, stupid and undesirable. Could it be true? Maybe that is why they keep telling me about the grotto. Maybe if I went there, it would make me desirable enough for someone to ask my family to marry me. If that happened, I could escape. That's it. I decided to do it.

And so the preparations began. Let's jump ahead two short weeks.

I have never been so nervous in my life. For years I have heard about this ritual, how it is performed, what I need to have with me and what I need to do. I never dreamed I would perform it myself. I am fully dressed in my jellaba and head scarf, as usual, but today I am carrying a red string with me. I only hope I can find at least one, preferably several older, married women to help me when I get there. My family has been so difficult lately that I decided I would have to do this without them, so I left school early today, before anyone would know I am gone.

I took the bus out to the river. Then, I hiked to where I was told to find the grotto, along the sea, a little ways past the mouth of the river. I made sure no one followed me.

When I got close to where I was told to go, I was lucky enough to find two old women. They were smiling and they asked me if I needed help with the ritual. I was very grateful. They helped me push past the crowd, which I did not expect to be there, and into the grotto. The sandy floor was soft and wet. They told me to get ready.

I took off all of my clothes and handed them to one of the women. The other one tied a red string to my wrist and told me to lay down on a long, flat rock in the corner, which she pointed out. I did. The women laughed and told me I did it wrong, and corrected how I was laying down.

They said that for the ritual to be effective, they have to leave me alone in the grotto, just as I am, and that they will exit, holding the other end of the red string. "How long to I have to stay here?" I asked.

"Just until we tug on the other end. We will do that when we are sure that the baraka is working. It may take half an hour or an hour. Just wait. Don't forget, you have to be completely silent the whole time."

So I laid there. And I laid there. And I laid there some more. Finally, it had been several hours. I knew because the sun was high in the sky when I entered, and now it was starting to get dark. I tugged on the string. It didn't give, and it didn't tug back. I got worried. What if the ritual didn't work? What would I do?

I heard voices outside, lots of them, mostly young men. Someone noticed the string moving. Oh no, they were laughing and talking. What was that they were saying? Something about another one duped. Where are the women? Where are my clothes? How will I ever get out of here?

Don't Cry

"Shut that child up, and do it now!" The voice echoed through the house, continuing up the narrow alley we lived on, and into the ears of our neighbors.

"Grandma, why do you have to be so loud and angry sounding when you say that?" I asked tentatively. "All the neighbors will hear, and it embarrasses me."

"I have to be loud, so that the neighbors know that we are doing our best to keep things quiet. I don't want them to think we are ignoring the boy. That would be worse."

"It doesn't matter anyway," I replied with a

sigh, "They can't hear what you are saying over all the screaming and crying. Grandma, we have to do something."

"I have an idea."

Slowly and deliberately, the old woman packed a small bag with food. She gently picked up her very loud grandson and motioned to her granddaughter to follow. The two of them walked through the ancient city of Fez together, winding through the twists and turns of narrow passages, past open areas with fountains and shops, down dark and forbidding alleys. Not a sound was spoken by either woman, but little Nassir cried loudly the entire way.

Finally, they exited the gate at Bab Ftouh.

"Grandma, where are we going?" the younger woman asked.

"We are going to get help from Sidi Harazem."

"Sidi Harazem!" the boy's mother replied, "Are you crazy? We don't have the money to take a bus all the way to the saint's hot springs."

"What do they teach children now days? Honestly, my granddaughter, do you not know that there are two saints with that name? The second, Sidi Harazem the Cold, is buried right up on the hill in front of you, on the way to Sahab al Ward. We can walk there in a few minutes."

The group walked, out from the city gate, across the large road that goes to the new town in one direction and to Oujda in the other, and began their trek up the hill on the other side. They passed the walls of the cemetery. They passed the vendors, with their wares on blankets on the curb. The grandmother stopped in front of a man with a cart loaded with fresh fruit. Nassir was still discontent and loud.

"How much for two oranges?" she asked.

Then followed some bargaining and arguing, until finally, she was content with the price and bought two big ones.

"I really don't understand what you are doing," chimed her granddaughter.

"We need an offering for the saint. Since we are poor, this will be acceptable."

"But, grandma, what are we doing?"

"Sidi Harazem the Cold is able to cure children of screaming and crying fits. This has been done for hundreds of years. Some people try to do it at home, but it is far more effective to do it here, at his tomb. Come, and you will understand."

They climbed further, eventually entering the gate to the cemetery. Then, they winded past the markers to the mausoleum of the saint. It looked like most, about ten or twelve feet square, with a green tile roof, and a metal door on one end. There was a person sitting on the step by the door, dressed in rags with a dirty face and matted hair.

"This, my granddaughter, is one of the descendants of Sidi Harazem, and so she must be honored. The family carries, to this day, a special blessing and power. The ladies gave their gift of fruit, which was gratefully accepted. Then, the door to the tomb was opened. Little Nassir was beside himself with frustration, loudly venting his anger with tears. The ladies entered the tomb, with their guide, and placed Nassir on the floor.

"Quickly, you must move quickly," their guide prodded.

All of them ran out of the door, except for the boy. The door to the tomb was shut and bolted from the outside. Nassir screamed even louder from within.

"How long do we have to do this?" the

child's mother begged. "I can't take it!"

Both the grandmother and the daughter of the saint replied that he must remain in the tomb until he is calm, completely calm. If he does, he will never cry again.

They waited. The screams changed from angry to frantic as panic took over.

"Grandma! He's only two!!"

"No, child, we must leave him there. The saint will help him."

The weeping mother listened as her son's tears turned from hysterical weeping to a mournful wail, and then to a whimper.

"Can we go in yet to get him?" she asked.

"No, not yet. He must be silent."

The ladies waited for over two hours. They ate some of the food they brought, sharing with their hostess. The mother cried some more and was held and consoled by the other two.

"There, there, dear. You really are doing the right thing. He will be so much better behaved after this is over."

Finally, it was silent. To be sure, the ladies waited another twenty or thirty minutes, asking Sidi Harazem to help the boy and make sure he would stay calm. Then they opened the door.

Looking up, they saw two glassy eyes with a distant stare. The treatment was effective. He would never cry again.

Epilogue

I have spent the last few weeks reading over my notes and this manuscript again. In the process, I found some photos; one of the fig tree mentioned in *A Wife from the Mountains*, another of me with the friend with whom I attended the soccer match, shots of various sites in the city of Fes, where I was privileged to live for many years, and several more.

During this time, I have been struck yet again by how normal all of these stories seemed to the people telling them. The supernatural was not something unusual or exotic to them, it simply described power beyond what each of them had.

Many of my friends in Morocco believe in these things. Many do not. All give assent to the prevalence of its existence in the corporate mindset. You can not have a conversation in Morocco without mentioning God. You can not greet your neighbor, welcome a client, or visit the barber without the name of God being invoked, typically many times. In Morocco, even the agnostics and the atheists speak of God, the devil, angels, demons, genies, blessings and curses. You can not understand the country nor the culture without first understanding both its official religion, Islam, and also its unofficial quasi-religious beliefs.

I am now living back in my country of origin, the United States of America. There are wonderful things in both places, but I find myself missing in America the openness that Moroccan culture has to the existence of the supernatural realm. Those who talk about such things in the West generally fall into the category of X-Files fans, UFO believers, or a certain percentage of religious adherents. In each case, the general population thinks these beliefs are eccentric; benign at best, odd and dangerous at worst.

Personally, I think our world could stand to have a bit more openness to mysticism, more of an acknowledgment that there are things that are unexplainable by science and which may best be left that way. Then again, perhaps the current trend toward movies with orcs, fairies, and religious themes are demonstrating a return of openness that is growing in the hearts and lives of the younger generations, no longer content to believe in nothing but that which may be proven or observed by the scientific method. Time will tell.

In any case, I hope you have enjoyed the book and have gained from it a new insight into and appreciation of a culture and people whom I love deeply.

Final notes and thoughts

You may have noticed the license under which I have released this work. Let me take a moment and explain why I have done this, rather than reserve all of the rights for myself. This work is definitely copyrighted, you can see that on one of the first pages. I am the copyright holder. I have created this work for several purposes, one of which is that I hope to make some money from it. However, this is not the only reason for publishing this book. My greatest hope is that other people will find the information contained within it useful. I have given you, the reader, permission to copy, distribute, display and perform this work, and to make derivative works, as long as you follow a few simple rules on which I will now comment.

First, you have to make sure and tell everyone that I am the author and owner of the copyright. In other words, you can copy it for your personal use or even for others to benefit from, but you can't claim that you are the author.

Second, you may not use this work for commercial purposes—that's my prerogative and my privilege alone as the creator of the work. I'm happy for you to use it as you like and even share it, but any money made from this work should be made by me.

Finally, if you alter, transform or build upon this work for any purpose other than personal use (that is, if you distribute your changes or additions) you must also release your work under this same license. You can be paid for your work, your additions or changes, but you have to let others use them in the same way I have let you use this work. Why?

It is my goal that as many people as possible benefit from this work. If you want to study it in a group and one person from the group buys a copy and then makes photocopies for the others in the group, I'm okay with that. If you can afford to, I would prefer that you each buy copies, but I'm not going to be persnickety about it as long as you don't sell the copies. I really hope that you will be able to make good use of the content that is in this work, that you feel free to discuss it, and learn from it.

I want you to feel free to make a study guide if you wish, or recordings of the texts, or whatever else you might think up. However, if you do so, then I simply require that you treat me and others as I have treated you. I require that you release your work with the same availability and limits I have placed on this one so that others will benefit from your work just as you have benefited from mine. I also ask that you properly cite your original source (me). Sound fair? I think so. "Freely you received, so freely give."

Following in the same vein as the work's license, all the software and even the fonts used in creating this book are freely licensed and can be used and distributed without cost.

Fonts used.

FreeSans and FreeSerif, Copyleft 2002, 2003, 2005 Free Software Foundation, www.gnu.org and www.fsf.org and directory.fsf.org/freefont.html for more information.

Also by Matthew Helmke

Humor and Moroccan Culture
ISBN: 978-0-6151-4284-5

Available on Amazon.com and may be ordered from most major retailers.

More of Matthew Helmke's writing can be found on his website at http://matthewhelmke.com/